THE QUEEN OF HEARTS

SING A SONG
FOR SIXPENCE

illustrated by
Randolph Caldecott

This edition is distributed by
AVENEL BOOKS
a division of Crown Publishers, Inc.

THE QUEEN OF HEARTS

THE QUEEN OF HEARTS.

THE Queen of Hearts,
She made some Tarts,

All on a Summer's Day:

The Knave of Hearts,
He stole those Tarts,

And took them right away.

The King of Hearts,
Called for those Tarts,

And beat the Knave full sore:

The Knave of Hearts,
Brought back those Tarts,

And vowed he'd steal no more.

SING A SONG
FOR SIXPENCE

Sing a Song for Sixpence,

A Pocketful

of Rye;

Four-and-Twenty Blackbirds

Baked

in a Pie.

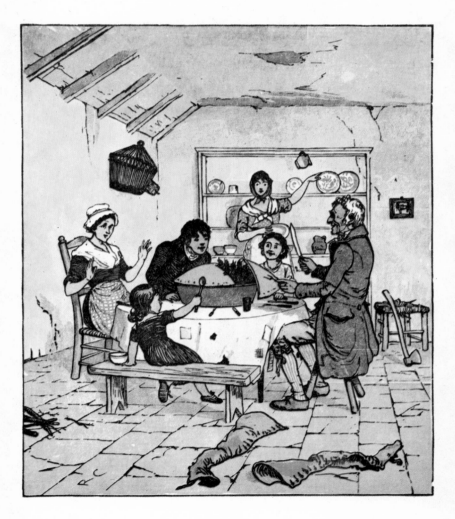

When the Pie was opened,
The Birds began to sing;

Was not that

a dainty Dish

To set before the King?

The King was in

his counting-house,

Counting out his Money.

The Queen was in

the Parlour,

Eating Bread and Honey.

The Maid was in

the Garden,

Hanging out the Clothes;

There came a little Blackbird,

And snapped off her Nose.

But there came a
Jenny Wren
and popped it on again.